THE PIED PIPER OF PERU

THE PIED PIPER OF PERU

BY ANN TOMPERT

ILLUSTRATED BY KESTUTIS KASPARAVICIUS

BOYDS MILLS PRESS

The publisher wishes to thank the Reverend Raymond Halligan, OP, of the Martin de Porres Guild, New York City, for his sound advice and careful reading of the manuscript. Further thanks to Brother Pius and the Dominicans of the Monastery of the Apostles Philip and James in Vilnius, Lithuania, for their generous assistance to Mr. Kasparavicius.

Published by Boyds Mills Press, Inc.
A Highlights Company
815 Church Street
Honesdale, Pennsylvania 18431
Printed in China
Visit our Web site at www.boydsmillspress.com

U.S. Cataloging-in-Publication Data
(Library of Congress Standards)

Tompert, Ann.
The Pied Piper of Peru / by Ann Tompert ; illustrated by Kestutis Kasparavicius. — 1st ed.
[32] p. : col. ill. ; cm.
Summary: The legend of Martin de Porres and how he rids a monastery of mice.
ISBN: 1-56397-949-7
1. Martin, de Porres, Saint, 1579-1639 — Juvenile literature. 2.
Christian saints — Peru — Juvenile literature. [1.Martin, de Porres,
Saint, 1579-1639. 2. Christian saints — Peru.] I. Kasparavicius,
Kestutis. II. Title.
270.6/ 092 [B] 21 2002 CIP
2001087635

First edition, 2002
The text of this book is set in 15-point Garamond.

10 9 8 7 6 5 4 3 2 1

To L. R. with heartfelt thanks
—A. T.

For my father
—K. K.

My NAME IS JUANA. For many
years I lived with a colony of mice in a priory in
Lima, Peru. We had a good life with the friars
who lived there. We found plenty of food in the
kitchen and pantry. We had snug little homes
in nearby nooks and crannies.

For a long time we lived in peace because we were careful, helping ourselves to no more food than we needed. Then, much to our sorrow, Luiz, who had an insatiable craving for cheese, joined our colony.

He gnawed great gaping holes in every wheel of cheese he could sniff out. Of course, it wasn't long before the damage was discovered.

"Mice are taking over the kitchen and pantry," I overheard Brother Fernando complain to the Prior.

"We must get a cat," said the Prior, who was head of the house.

The next day Pizarro, a monstrous cat, came
to the priory. He nosed about our nooks and
crannies and relentlessly patrolled the kitchen
and pantry, seeking mice to devour.

"We are not safe here," said my mother.

"We must move," said my father.

Thus it was that our family, taking all our
earthly possessions, fled with the rest of the colony.
    One by one, we migrated to the linen closets,
wardrobes, and trunks, and settled in.

    Although we rationed our food carefully, it
soon was gone. Several times my father and I
tried to work our way past the constantly watchful
Pizarro. But he blocked our every move.

To ward off hunger, we made soup from bits and pieces of sheets and blankets and clothing. My father and I were forced to harvest leather from a belt.

"We must find food or we'll starve," I said.

The next day I decided to explore the priory.
"Surely," I thought, "there must be food
somewhere other than in the kitchen and pantry."
I was creeping along a wall when suddenly
I heard voices. I peeked around the corner. The
Prior and Brother Martin were on their way to
see Brother Fernando.

"Look at this," said Brother Fernando.
He held out a sheet riddled with holes.

"Mice," said the Prior.

"Poor creatures," said Brother Martin.
"They are hungry. No one feeds them."

"That may be, Martin," said the Prior.
"But you are to get rid of them."

"Pizarro is not the answer," said Brother
Fernando. "He'll only chase them someplace else."

"Traps, then," said the Prior. "Or poison."

Brother Martin bowed silently and slipped
away. Hugging the wall, I followed behind him.
I hoped to learn what he planned to do. I was
surprised to find him sweeping the floor. Surely,
he didn't intend to sweep us away. The thought
made me smile in spite of my anxiety.

Hiding in the shadows, I heard only the sound of Martin's broom swishing over the stone floor. Then he began to murmur to himself. I inched closer to hear better.

"What am I going to do?" he said. "I must obey the Prior's order. But I can't harm these creatures of God. If only I could talk to them."

In my eagerness to hear every word, I grew careless and crept closer and closer until Brother Martin caught sight of me. He leaned toward me. I turned to run.

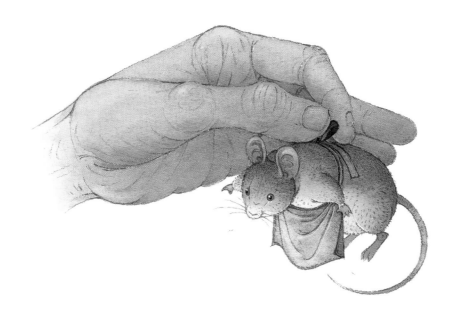

"Hello, my little friend," he said.

My deep-seated instinct was to flee, but I couldn't. Something in his gentle voice made me pause.

He picked me up.

I should have trembled with fear. But I didn't. I should have jumped to safety. But I didn't. Somehow I was not afraid. Sitting in Brother Martin's cupped hand and gazing into his dark eyes, I felt as safe as a mousling in a nest of clover.

"Now, listen carefully," he said. "You mice are doing great harm to our linens and clothes. The Prior is not pleased. You all must leave the priory. If you move to the barn, I will bring you food every day. Do you understand?"

I nodded.

Brother Martin carefully placed me down on the floor, and I scurried away.

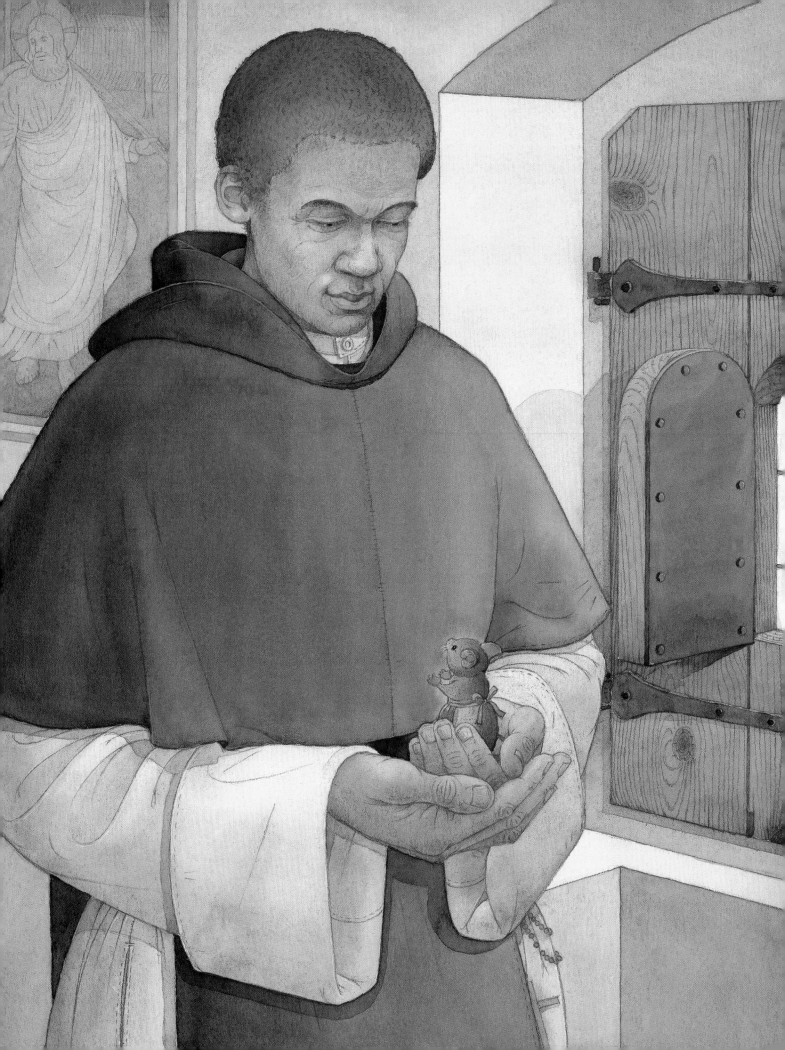

Moments later, I was rushing about announcing the good news. Most of the mice were skeptical and suspicious.

"Sounds too good to be true," said one.

"It's a trap," said another.

"Pizarro and an army of cats will be waiting to capture us," said a third.

"But we'll starve to death if we stay," I said.

"We'll just have to hope for the best," said my father.

I could see that I'd never persuade them with words. Action was necessary.

I peeked into the hall. At first all I saw was Martin. All I heard was his swishing broom. Then I spied two fierce green eyes glowing in the shadows near a bench. Pizarro was waiting. My heart stopped. I hesitated. "It's now or never," I thought.

And I dashed out to Martin.

We met at Martin's feet. I felt Pizarro's cruel claws grab me. I heard his tail whipping back and forth. I closed my eyes and held my breath, waiting for the fatal blow.

"Stop," said Martin quietly.

Pizarro dropped me like a piece of red-hot iron. Martin leaned over and whispered in his ear.

Pizarro slowly turned and crept away. But he lashed his tail and glanced back at me several times. I wondered if that would be the last I'd see of him.

"Where are the others?" Martin asked.

As if answering his question, a rustling sound like dry leaves stirred by the wind soon filled the air as all of the mice abandoned their homes.

Mice popped out from under wardrobes and trunks.

Mice scrambled from the joists in the ceiling and the cracks in the floors.

It wasn't long before a small army of mice rallied at Martin's feet.

I marched by Martin's side as he led us down a series of long halls. At every turn I expected to confront Pizarro. We had almost reached the priory door when I spied his eyes glowing in the shadows. Slowly they moved toward us. I looked about wildly for an escape route.

Just as the cat prepared to pounce, Martin said, "Here's Pizarro come to bid you safe journey."

Pizarro froze in his tracks. And he watched as we paraded out the priory door.

We soon set up housekeeping in the barn.
    And, true to his word, Martin brought food to
us every day. In gratitude, not one mouse ever
set paw into the priory again.

ABOUT MARTIN DE PORRES

The Pied Piper of Peru was inspired by accounts of an incident in the life of Saint Martin de Porres, who was born in Lima, Peru, on December 9, 1579. His father was a Spanish nobleman and his mother a freed African slave. He was twelve years old when he was apprenticed to Doctor de Rivero. He soon showed a remarkable ability to heal the sick and wounded.

Three years later, when he was fifteen, Martin joined the Holy Rosary Priory of the Dominican Friars in Lima. There he worked as a lay helper. He became a Dominican lay brother when he was twenty-two.

Martin was credited with many of what were considered miraculous cures. Numerous people from Lima, rich and poor, flocked to the priory seeking his help. He provided hundreds of people with food and clothing. He founded an orphanage, a hospital, schools, and a home for young unmarried women.

Martin helped animals as well as people. Besides the tale told here, there are many other stories of Martin's interaction with animals.

When Martin died on November 3, 1639, everyone who knew him considered him a saint. But his canonization (the process by which the Catholic Church names someone a saint) met with many delays and setbacks. It was not until 1962 that the Church declared Martin a saint.